# Love Is Blind in One Eye

*7 Stories*

Marianne Rogoff

To:

From:

*Love Is Blind in One Eye*.

Shebooks
3060 Independence Avenue
Bronx, NY 10463
Visit our website at www.Shebooks.net

Shebooks is a trademark of First Persona, LLC.

ISBN: 978-1-940838-84-7

First Edition: May 2016

## Dedication

To my son

You have brains in your head.
You have feet in your shoes.
You can steer yourself in any direction you choose.
You're on your own, and you know what you know.
And you are the one who'll decide where to go.
– Dr. Seuss

Praise for Marianne Rogoff

"I loved reading these seven stories and spending time with Jewel. A curious, bold, sensual, and tender young woman, she pursues her adventures in Maui, Mexico, Marin, Lisbon, and Barcelona with light, sure steps."

– Molly Giles, Author of The Spokane Prize story collection *All the Wrong Places* and The Flannery O'Connor Award for Short Fiction collection *Rough Translations*

\* \* \*

"This is one beautiful book. I loved and devoured it–like candy, like medicine. Rogoff had me by the throat and the heart from first page to last. These extraordinary stories will stay with me for a very long time. What a gorgeous, devastating, liberating collection. Just perfect."

– Lavinia Spalding, Author of *Writing Away* and Editor of *The Best Women's Travel Writing*

\* \* \*

"Marianne's compelling yet simply told stories gently take our hand and lead us through moments of tragedy and daily triumph that could easily be our own as parents, as travelers, and as friends, and ultimately reveal the indelible strength of character and vulnerability that make us all human beings."

– Kimberley Lovato, Travel Journalist and Author of *Walnut Wine & Truffle Groves*

\* \* \*

"Rogoff's writing is rife with an emotional acuity that is riveting; carved out of a fierce knowing of what it is to navigate - and survive - life on life's terms. Deliciously poignant, the stories collected here are both raw and sophisticated, masterfully interwoven to reveal how one forges ahead with resilience and grace while on the precipice of a vast chasm of grief. An astounding, beautiful work."

– Bridget Crocker, Outdoor Travel Writer/Blogger: *adventuresoflittlemama.com*

# Table of Contents

**7 Stories**

*Introduction*

# Introduction

This linked collection is part truth, part fiction. I personally did not walk on fire or find a body on a beach but a co-worker I knew did both, and as I wrote her story it felt like my own; I began to identify with the woman walking, with Jewel's desire to confront her fears then to let them go, "into the fire."

Jewel is an alter ego, "a second self, a trusted friend, the opposite side of a personality." Travel offers a chance to try on new versions of yourself that you put on when you arrive and leave behind as you depart. Coming home, you reassess who you thought you were before you left and who you really are, or want to be. But this kind of internal shift can erupt anywhere, even at home, as you explore foreign emotions, or recognize what is extraordinary and always mysterious about everyday life wherever you are.

Here, Jewel navigates the stage of life between 25 and 45, from the day she finds a body on a wild California beach to crossroads encounters with mystics, lovers, beggars, surgeons, and sailors on the shores of Maui and streets of San Miguel de Allende, Lisbon, Larkspur, Mill Valley, and Barcelona. Falling in love, whether with the one she marries, her newborn babies, total strangers, or the places she goes, calls forth conflicting sensations: ease/excitement, pleasure/danger, attachment/release.

One eye sees and the other is blind as Jewel learns to love and grieve by staying in motion, finding and losing her way in the crowds and landscapes, heart cracked open.

## Firewalking

The air is unseasonably hot for this stretch of northern California beach in June, where everyone expects the fog in summer to keep it cool. Then only the tourists are caught off-guard in their short shorts while the locals always carry sweaters in anticipation of the chill. This morning I am out walking RCA beach early and there is no fog; the view is clear for miles. The sun is up and I'm already sweating which is why I walk fast: I like to sweat. My body is tall and strong as I pick my way over rocks around bends where the tide, when it is in, consumes the beach, leaving no passage. For now the tide is low and leaves pools with pink edges and starfish, swaying circular fingers holding on tight that are like flowers and animals at the same time. There are tiny crabs, and kelp.

RCA is a wild, empty beach because it is so hard to reach. But I had walked easily across the meadow, then shimmied the steep rocky trail down to this place that mostly only townies know how to get to, and usually only surfers bother to hike the difficult path. Seven AM, no surfers, one figure carrying a fishing pole walking toward me. I'm not even thirty (I'm young!) but there are times when I feel every step I've ever taken down rocky paths in the bones of my knees. This morning I don't. I squeeze my flesh and think I should go on a diet, then assure myself this body cushions me as I move along the craggy beach, confident about my feet and knees, how strong I feel and take deep breaths and stop to examine a seashell that looks like a small breast, the way it curls to a center with a shining tip, the way it is round and so extravagant looking there in the sand.

The fisherman stops in front of me.

"There's a body over there," he says, and I

look into his white bucket in which three silver sea bass float, eyes wide, not seeing. The man explains where the body is; he is on his way to call someone. He's wearing hip waders, shuffling awkwardly with his gear, and does not say much except how surprised he was when as he was fishing he saw it from the water. He expected another dead seal or sea otter, he says, because of the size of the mound. But as he waded in he noticed this glinting off the surface of the water, then saw that the shining came from a ring on a woman's hand.

"It's not a pretty sight," he says as he walks away. "You might want to turn around right here."

*I have walked on fire. I have no fear.*

I keep going forward, in the same direction.

\* \* \*

Five years earlier I went along as the photographer for my reporter boyfriend Lee when he was researching his *Pacific Sun* article on firewalkers. I was 25, maybe 24, and we were happy, in love, oblivious, laughing at the whole idea on the way over in the car.

"Any mother would tell her child not to walk

barefoot over hot coals," Lee said, and I agreed, walking on fire sounded like a crazy thing to do.

We sat there smug as the group gathered into a circle and we were told to introduce ourselves.

"I'm Jewel," I began….

"Without words," the leader ordered. I had to think about how to do that, and then I smiled and shrugged.

As the sun dropped behind Mount Tamalpais I listened and watched the others, and found I had to take my camera away from my face because Simone was not one of those silly New Age California types you hear so much about. We had joined a group of seekers not so different from us: reticent, easygoing men and women we liked on instinct. In the glow of everything Lee and I basked in our passionate love, arrogant, certain of our glorious future.

We all sat cross-legged in the dark around a blazing fire of hardwood and embers and Simone instructed us to write down our fears.

"The first part is to name your fear."

*Loving Lee, losing Lee.*

"Next is to banish it."

Simone told us to crumple the lists into tight balls and throw them in the fire.

I kept looking at my list – *loving Lee, losing Lee* – afraid to admit either possibility, then I watched the fears of the others shrivel into smoke, so I freely let mine go, too, up in flames.

Now, Simone raked the fire out from its neat round heap into a long bed of red coals, about ten feet from end to end.

"It's five quick steps," she said.

One. Two. Three. Four. Five.

"You have all that fear and you feel the heat for less than ten seconds. The fear is taking up more of your time than the thing you fear."

\* \* \*

My toes tighten inside my sneakers on the beach as the waves roll toward me. The sun has risen fully now over the steep cliff where sand and stones are ever-eroding, slipping down the hillside in a constant musical cadence much like the rhythm of the ocean that swallows the beach and reaches the cliff at high tide, twice a day.

*Dead body? Here? On this beautiful beach?*

\* \* \*

Simone firewalking had slipped out of her shoes, stepped onto the hot bed of embers, and walked in a regular pace, five steps from end to end, across the coals.

Lee had declined, unconvinced, but I'd felt enlivened, bold, then fearless: I walked on fire.

\* \* \*

*I have no fear.*

The corpse is face-up on the sand, seawater crashing around her feet and legs. Her clothes are torn; skin dry, purple, bruised; neck and arms twisted; deep gashes on her thighs; fists clenched. She's blonde, around my age (!), and the look on her face, in contrast to the shape of her body, is serene. Her eyes are open, as calm as the fish in the fisherman's bucket.

\* \* \*

After firewalking everyone else had soaked their feet in big pails of cold water but my feet had felt fine as I made portraits of newfound friends. We all wrote declarations on index cards: "I have walked on fire. I can do anything."

Mine is pinned to a bulletin board in my kitchen now but I want to turn around like the fisherman said and leave this woman to her fate in someone else's presence, not mine. On the way home from the firewalking my feet felt burning hot. By the time Lee had driven us back home over the mountain, blisters had formed all over the soles of my feet, most painfully in the arches. I stoically stripped off my socks and said, "They're just little blisters, they'll be gone in the morning."

But by morning I could barely walk.

\* \* \*

*The tide is coming in. The fisherman has not returned. The body is floating in and out on the waves.*

\* \* \*

I recall a Raymond Carver story where a group of men go on a weekend fishing trip and discover the body of a woman near the shore of the river, tangled in branches. Far from phones or civilization, having just driven a long way, they decide it's not their problem; they're tired; they have come to fish. The men play cards and drink whiskey; they sleep, wake, fish, drink, and eat; the dead woman remains in the river downstream from where they fish and they don't report her death until the end of the weekend.

When the narrator's wife hears the story she's outraged.

"That woman needed you," she tells her husband.

*If I take no action, this body will be swept back and forth by the tide and she may be here when the fisherman returns with help or she may not.*

I remember the morning in my childhood when my mother urged me to kiss my dead grandmother goodbye and how awful it was to learn how unyielding the dead are to touch, like stones or walls. How my blistered feet burned after firewalking, how painful it was to stand on the bottoms of my own feet, how Lee mocked me as I became an old lady who had to walk with a cane, leaning on that stick like a third leg.

\* \* \*

*I was fearless then. Now I am afraid.*

Reluctantly, cautiously, then boldly, I touch her. Tenderly, I unwrap sea kelp from around the throat then dare to outline the lips with a fingertip. The skin is rubbery, strange, not alive; no blood pulses, but she's not bones or ashes yet. I examine the ears: dried peach halves dehydrated by salt water. Diamond stud earrings, what will become of them? I fondle the gems then the face: bruised cheek, crushed forehead. The eyes stare; I stick my finger on her eyeball (peeled grapes) and no one blinks.

Do the wounds suggest she was killed then left on this remote beach to float unnoticed out to sea? Or did she get here on her own volition, by jumping off the famous bridge? The beautiful body has scraped past all obstacles and rests beside me here in the sand. Getting acquainted without words, I hold hands with the dead. As I imagine her life, I foresee my own future: high tides and crumbling losses. I come to know my own death.

Waves splash and spill foam so I slide my forearms under the shoulders to move her farther up on shore, but she is too heavy to move. Now I know the meaning of dead weight. The tide rides her hips. I don't want the body taken by the ocean. She needs to be here to be found. I stay with her and wait.

## Someplace Else

### *Mirage*

When I told my mother I was going on vacation to Maui with my husband and two-year-old, she mentioned plane crash, volcano, and tidal wave.

"Do you not want me to go?" I asked.

"Oh no, go. Have a good time."

Our first afternoon there, while Lee and Dale were napping, I read *Guide to Maui,* and there it was: tsunami, "a very real threat." We had just flown over from San Francisco, earthquake country. How prepared should we be? Do we need flashlights, canned food, batteries, a radio?

The *Guide* said, "Go to higher ground immediately when you hear the bell sound." What would I take with me, besides my baby boy? What was valuable, worth risking time to save? I.D. cards, so someone would call my mother if I died, and money, in case we survived on higher ground while everything left behind was lost. Since being robbed last time we were on vacation I now left my most sentimental jewelry at home, although our empty house, I always thought, was as good a target as a hotel room or rented car.

I left Lee a note and slipped out for a swim. The owner had warned us about the sharp, cutting coral when we arrived. "Pick your feet up and start swimming right away," the old guy with his arm in a sling told us, "That's the ticket."

I stepped through breaking waves and dove lightly onto the water's surface, then turned over and floated face-up; I let go and the shallow ocean held me up. I swam. Alone. Felt myself, judged my body, good, stroking muscles through water, taking deep breaths, floating on the aqua sea. Swam out far from shore, strong, aware of my strength. Then a bright yellow fish startled me. In its light brightness I saw the soul of my firstborn, and yearned for her, *I thought you were dead,* forcing my arms and torso through thick waves, faltering as the so-bright color disappeared in the dark reefs. The stark brightness swam far away and there was the stark truth: *Silvie IS dead.* I suffocated under this fact, weakened, struggling to save myself from whirlpools and undertows, down-sucking emptiness, the watery tide shoving me along to land and air: safe, only my baby girl was gone.

I lay on my back onshore as a gust of wind ransacked the beach. I sat up: wind-blown sand in my mouth; in the distance, Lee and Dale. Dale was two; Lee and I had survived more than two years with Silvie dead. Time so reliably passing while we lagged behind in our baby girl's nascence and eternity, out of step with the fast necessary pace of living.

Our perfect son meanwhile moved swiftly across the beach, deft and well balanced, regaining his footing quickly after dips and changes in the shifting land. Then he made a beeline for the ocean. Here, the water was a bay, and calm. But the smallest wave would knock him down. He was so little, vulnerable, brave, and foolhardy: oblivious to danger. We wanted him to feel safe but our next job as parents was to alert him to danger. Edges, waves, thorns, strangers with bad intentions. Plane crash, volcano, tidal wave.

*Vacation*

Lee and I walked past the open windows of

our vacation neighbors and we could see them on the couch watching TV and drinking shots over ice from a half gallon of dark liquor.

"Probably bourbon," Lee said.

"I'm glad we're not them," I decided, and Lee agreed, "I'm glad we're not drunks."

We were on vacation in Maui. We had hired a sitter for Dale and were going out on a date, to a seafood place on the water. What we planned to do besides eat, we didn't know, we were just walking, so far.

"We could be very comfortable in a place like this if we had the money," I said.

"We *are* in a place like this," Lee pointed out.

I was wearing a new pink silk blouse, an expensive one, imported from Paris.

"I'll act like we're rich and comfortable, for you, because we're here."

Alone at the restaurant without our baby boy, we talked about how much we loved him, admired him.

"We're lucky," Lee said.

*There are the boats rocking on the water.*
*The moon is full.*

*Look, first star.*
*Palm trees.*

"I don't feel like myself," I said.

"Who do you feel like?"

"Here we are on this island. God." I pulled a fishbone from my mouth.

"Aren't you having a good time, Jewel?" Lee asked.

"I'm not sure."

"I feel lost, too, as lost as you do."

When we left the restaurant it was drizzling and we walked in the mist past tied-up, rocking boats to the bar at the end of the harbor. Most people in there seemed drunk; it felt like a locals place, like they'd come straight from work to here and spent the afternoon, now evening. At a table near us, a guy was lining up empty beer bottles in a winding spiral that ended at the center with a full ashtray.

"What do you want?" Lee asked me.

He ordered rum and pineapple juice.

I said, "Ever since Silvie died, it's like I'm wrapped in gauze. I'm numb. I need to come back to my senses."

"That's why we're here."

Two women came in and sat at the bar. I saw them as the one who lived here and the visiting friend. They were about my age, between 29 and 35, out on a Friday night, dressed down but feminine touches caught your eye. The visiting friend wore a denim jacket, but her white skirt was inviting. The one who lived here, her sparkly red tee shirt was tucked in tight in her jeans and she seemed to know all the men.

One guy yelled over for her and her friend to join him and his friends. She argued a few minutes across the room then joined them. I drank rum with Lee, which was expensive. An older, beautiful woman in a flowered dress came in selling flowers and leis.

"I'd get you one of those if you wanted," Lee said.

I considered it while one of the drunks waved the flower lady over and bought scented leis for the two women. They pushed their heads through the necklaces, put the flowers to their noses, and smelled. I could smell gardenia from way over here. *Could it please me to have one of those leis as much as it pleased those two?* They smiled in their gardenia garlands and posed for pictures. The drunk man got up on a chair with the visiting friend's camera and aimed down at the whole table of men and the two women wearing their leis until the waitress came along and told him to keep his feet on the floor or he'd have to leave.

"Maybe we could go someplace else?" Lee suggested, draping me with gardenia flowers.

The wind blew my flowing pink skirt up as we came down stairs from the second-floor bar and my husband wrapped an arm around me as we stepped outside into heavy rain that was fierce and wet, but warm. He pulled me close and we walked hip against hip past the fishing boats. Guiding me by the waist, Lee steered us under the awning of Maalea general store, to a bench where we sat out of the downpour; for a few minutes quietly we watched the rain fall and keep falling.

I sniffed the lei and said, "I feel like a fool." Lee watched my shadowy face for clues. "For being here." I moved closer to him. "No one else seems to worry about how much everything costs."

"Are we talking about money? Now? Now that we're here?"

"You've always been cavalier about money."

"Don't use words like 'cavalier' in my presence, please." Lee said it jokingly, but tightened his lips and tucked his arms between his legs. I began to badger him about our lack of financial security, the F word. We were out on a date, on vacation, in Maui, HERE, fighting about money. I could hear that clinking sound that sailboats make in the wind, and smell jasmine in the air, salt water, and everything else sweet and indefinable. There was the beam of light on the water from the moon, and my husband's fingers combing my hair. Rain off the edge of the awning, dense, like a waterfall.

Lee said, "We could go back to the room."

"Not yet."

His lips sucked rain off my cheeks.

"What do you want?" His fingers twined mine on my leg and squeezed.

"I don't know why I thought there was anywhere I could go."

*"You can't run away from yourself,"* he sang the line as Bob Marley would have, soulfully, knowingly. My blouse clung to my breasts and Lee's wet arm beside me, the hair on it, caressed my bare arm. This close wetness, that's what marriage feels like: clasped fingers, woven threads.

"I want Silvie to be alive," I said.

"She's not."

"I know."

"We have Dale."

"And this is a very, very good thing. I love him so much more than I can say."

We held hands, then stood and started walking slowly on the path along the row of beachfront condos. My earrings twisted and turned against my neck in the wind so I took them off and carried them: seashells, worry stones.

"Remember when we took Silvie to your brother's wedding in Arizona?" Lee said. I didn't say anything and he went on, telling that story. "She was brain-dead, dying, but we didn't know when?" His legs were long, his pace grew quick and long; I kept up, walking beside him, his stride as familiar to me as my own.

"I was pregnant with Dale."

"We had a whole plan worked out with her doctor. If she looks like she's dying for real, he told us, just head for home. Don't say anything to anybody...."

"... because then there'd be medical heroics, futile interventions, all the wrong questions." I felt the fist in my lungs, right back there again, in the heat of that terrible trip.

"We did all that when she was born. We tried to save her. We loved her so much." Lee comforted me like always, his strong arm around me, holding my shoulders upright as we walked.

"There was no way to bring her to life, everyone knew it. But we all tried, day after day, for weeks, months."

"Dr. Whitelaw told us, 'Go to your brother's wedding. If Silvie dies on the road, protect her body in a cooler with ice if the desert gets too hot.' Insane advice, right?"

"At the California border agriculture check, we'd say, 'No fruit, Sir, just our dead baby.'"

"I remember that trip."

"I kept complaining that it didn't seem like much of a vacation."

"Yeah?"

"You said, 'Don't expect so much. We're just here to look at things in a different light.'"

We walked through the warm Hawaiian storm while our tears flowed side by side then dried in the rain, and we arrived at our door. We stood on cement and looked at each other in the dark. We could hear the wild surf pounding the beach, wind rattling palms, and our beating hearts. Lee kissed me, wet, hard, rapturously, and our slippery flesh pressed close in passion.

"Are you sorry we're here?" I asked.

"No, Babe, I'm glad we're here."

### Ambition

Every morning, a lone man cleaned the pool. Lee watched him through the window early, as the sun was coming up. The man was handsome, well built, in his forties maybe, barefoot with shorts, tee shirt, hat, and sunglasses that reflected whatever he faced. Systematic, slow, he appeared thoughtful, contented, as he worked, at the same hour every morning. First he hosed flower petals from the cement, then watered the lawn and landscaped bushes and plants, then turned to the chairs. He re-arranged them the same way each morning: two lounge chairs poolside, four chairs around the glass table, two chairs and a low table facing the beach, two *chaise longues* in the center of the little lawn. As the day's sunlight moved toward noon, everything would get moved around by sunbathers, to accommodate their shifting needs as they turned to face the sun at this or that point in the day. Or moved out of the sun to sit side by side in the shade of the palm. Lee watched out the window as the man did his job, before anyone else was up in the morning, alone, quietly, consistently. Did the man lack ambition? Or, was it possible, he had what he wanted? Stability. Peace. No expectations. No grief.

### The Rest of Our Lives

Dale was obsessively drawn to hats, and wherever he turned, it seemed, someone was wearing one. "Hat, hat," he would say, his first word.

There was a big, fat lady on the big beach wearing a white visor. Her legs were huge and dimpled, breasts mountainous; folds of herself wrapped around her as she rested on a striped beach towel in the palm-tree shade.

Dale ran up to her, said, "hat, hat," and she sat up and smiled at him.

"Cute," she said. "How old?"

"Two," I said, and Dale toddled off down the sand, with Lee following close beside him.

"Your first?" the big lady asked.

I gulped.

"No."

She looked around for the other.

We were on a magnificent beach, Makena; most people called it Big Beach. The sand was white and soft and stretched far away along the edge of the island where long waves of turquoise water lapped it.

"Our first baby died," I told her.

The woman was probably in her fifties. Now she sat up fully and tilted her eyes up from under the visor to see me better.

"I lost one, too," she said and patted the space beside her for me to sit with her.

Lee had wandered off toward the water with Dale. I could see them walking in that slow way you walk with toddlers, stopping and going, standing still for a second to study tiny bits of nature buried in the sand, then running to save him from danger as waves crashed toward him, over and over.

"My fifth out of seven," the woman said. "The rest of them are here with me, matter of fact. They're around somewhere, there." She waved to an approaching trio of grown sons. "What happened to yours?" she asked.

"Brain damage."

"My sixth has Down syndrome. The most beautiful child I have. She's rare; you should see her: skinny, blonde. Gorgeous, until she opens her mouth."

She considered her daughter's beauty, pictured it, cherished it then asked me. "Your baby full term?"

"Yes."

"Yes. My boy was eight pounds, eight ounces,

just fine. You'd never know anything was wrong. Two days after he was born he turned blue. Five days and he was dead. You know what it was? He had no chambers of the heart. Nowadays, God, they can even give you a new one. But then…." She went back over it in her mind and I could see the emotions heave in her chest, twenty years since she lost him.

She looked at me, "You know what I think happened?"

"What?"

"You know how the heart is formed sometime there in the early months?"

"Yes."

"I was given a shot and it went against nature. Do you know what happened to yours?"

"Not really. Loss of oxygen, maybe."

"During labor?"

"We think so."

"Live long?"

"Seven and a half months."

"How bad?"

"As bad as you can be and still be alive." Big Mama waited for me and I told her, "Silvie couldn't eat, cry, or grow."

"Couldn't grow? Imagine that."

Blue Hawaiian waves lapped sand over there, and the mama shifted back, following the shadow of the tree in the sand, closer to me, farther from the water as the tide rose and shadows shifted. Her big sons arrived and hunted through the cooler for beer then plopped down in the sandy boundary of territory the family had staked out.

"It's best she died, if it was that bad." Big Mama told me, without hesitation, certain it was true.

I could see Dale on the sunny beach, running to his father, who lifted him high in the air. My baby boy squealed with joy.

"There's reasons," Mama stated, as if to conclude and clarify everything. She gathered her huge body together, leaned on a knee and a three-footed cane, shifted her weight onto the sturdy cooler, sat, and placed her legs apart, assuming a solid stance. Her two daughters and three sons sprawled in the sand around her feet could have been an audience before the Sphinx, their mother one of Picasso's sculpted women, enigmatic like that, statuesque.

"There *are* reasons," she repeated, and I waited. "We just don't know what they are."

Mothers serve divine purposes. Just as some children are born to live on long after you and I are gone, those babies were meant to come and go before us, like waves, like drops of water into waves, passing through on the way to some place as far and unknown as the one from which, with such hard labor and innocent expectation, they emerged. We are merely vehicles, witnesses to predestined lives.

I stayed behind on the sand when Big Mama stood to go. She smiled and tilted her visor higher, leaning on faith, a cane, and her own two legs. She left the beach with the rest of her children, moving on to their next destinations: Waikiki, Las Vegas, then Florida, home.

### Waianapanapa

Lee and I marveled every day at our son, amazed, he came from nothing, a dot, a mysterious binding product of ourselves, which grew. His complexity was perfect, he contained everything he needed to become himself and move on.

We hiked with Dale in Lee's backpack-for-babies on one side of the state park, following signs to the burial site of an old king. The trail ran along the rough jagged cliffs of northeast Maui, and became more rocky as we went, waves breaking close, hard, and high.

The destination turned out to be a pile of rocks cemented together, with the king's long Hawaiian name handwritten in concrete, a monument to his life. What number of men had it taken to bury him here? How had they carried him? Like Elizabeth Taylor as Cleopatra, I pictured, on a pallet resting on the shoulders of his followers, men sweating in tropical sunshine as they struggled with the weight and walked the difficult path in search of sacred ground.

This king, so long dead, exuded nothing human; unlike a new death, in whose presence breathing life could still be felt, the king's body had already, centuries ago, been assimilated in the land. The world prevailed: vast sea crashing on black sand and sharp rocks, the dominion of God ceaselessly re-creating it. That old king had merged long ago with the earth where we stood; no longer separate from nature like we were, balanced precariously on the edge of an island. Midday. Sun high in the sky. Air warm on our shoulders, pulse in our throats, hearts pumping. Alive in earthly paradise.

Lee moved away, physical body, driven by breath and fluids, muscles rubbing on bones. He reached to hold my hand, sweaty as he carried our boy on his back, returning carefully along the trail, thirsty and hot. When Dale fell asleep he looked heavier, his head resting against the back of his father's neck, forcing Lee to hunch his own head forward.

"What a life," a stranger said, on the path. She nodded toward our sleeping prince. "Beautiful, too bad they have to grow up."

I knew what she meant: *This too shall pass; this beauty will pass.*

But to change was nature. We wanted him to grow.

Only spirit is lasting: the soul that precedes birth, sustains life, and transcends physical death. We can feel whole again aware of that presence, not empty, reverent, knowing life once born is everlasting; the proof was here, wild and intangible, everywhere around us.

We moved past the stranger, following signs to a former temple of worship on the other side of Waianapanapa, and arrived at another pile of rocks. We sat awhile on the ground against it. The view was grand. Then we turned around and hiked our way back to where we started.

## Emporio Rulli

First time I noticed Harry was because he had a copy of *The Rebel* balanced on the ledge next to his table at the café. It was the same paperback version with big orange letters that I had read in college. We all read Camus in college but I'd never seen a middle-aged man with a copy. Turned out we were Rulli regulars. I generally sat with a different crowd, though there were overlapping, smiling acquaintances with shared aptitude for the lifestyle. We came for the caffeine but mostly to participate in ongoing conversations that had no goal.

One morning I was up and out early and Harry was there at the café alone, dividing his attention between *Cliff Notes* (!) for *Steppenwolf* (Hermann Hesse), a cappuccino, a notepad where he made notes, and roving judgmental blue eyes all over each person who came through the door.

I was compelled to comment: "Cliff Notes?"

"Short and sweet," he tossed me the yellow and black striped pamphlet.

It landed in my creamy pastry.

He gestured that I should eat the cream.

I scooped a mouthful off the book then licked my fingers.

We smiled.

According to *Cliff Notes,* Steppenwolf disdained all evidence of human hunger and violence, hated beastliness, and especially abhored its presence in himself. He preferred to see himself as refined, like the denizens of Emporio Rulli. We knew better than to bring unseemly problems here, into space reserved for esoteric discourse. There was to be no talk that required taking sides or resolution. Gripes between used-to-be friends, over business, money, car deals, divorces, etcetera, were left outside. Though on any given day our reliable ease could be jarred (shockingly) by the appearance in our midst of a beast. The gracious upbeat intellectuals would quiet down for long staring moments as we reckoned with its uninvited presence: a crying baby, who doesn't understand the etiquette for making gross needs known. Or toddlers, who won't sit still, and like to climb walls. Teenagers dressed too sloppy (the guys) or too skimpy (the girls). Someone curses, too loud, another spills coffee all over someone's pressed beige suit.

\* \* \*

One afternoon Steppenwolf came in wearing a blonde wig under a Giants baseball hat. (I recognized him: I was reading the novel.) The beast was in a good mood, snapping his fingers, whistling. He wanted another glass of red wine, more, wine for everyone here. He moved to kiss a woman who didn't want to be kissed, dropped a glass and broke it, picked up a shard and made a gash across his wrist. Then he was bleeding in front of us and said something about heartache, bellyache, boredom, futility, fear, what else (fill in the blank...).

Harry noted, "Jewel, look up from your book, this is a true moment."

I looked around.

"You like spilled guts in public?"

Harry swept his arm around the room, gesturing at the bleeding man amidst the marble, mural, mirrors, coffee, cakes, and conversations, saying, "We love our pleasantries.... But we're also self-loathing saps and cruel brutes who commit atrocities."

    \* \* \*

Harry and I chatted at the cafe for months and never discussed our work, marital status, children, or where we came from; only our deepest literary tastes and thoughts on philosophy, art, music, sports, beauty, politics, and other trivial matters. Acquaintances, we only knew the stories we told in public and what we could guess because we read the same books. We weren't lovers. We were not even friends. But when I ran into Harry at Emporio Rulli we talked. One day I suddenly felt like telling him my cliché and we had this dialog about Lee.

"My husband wants a divorce," I said.

"Your husband is suffering," Harry was certain.

"I doubt it," I was equally sure.

"He has terrible guilt."

"He should!"

"He has no choice."

"Of course he has choice!"

Harry said affairs were no more than the "uncontrollable urge to flee."

"I love Lee. I thought I knew him."

"We never really know anyone."

"Not even ourselves...."

"We fall in love to love ourselves."

"So, all the mirrors in *Steppenwolf?*"

"He sees himself in every one; every character he meets shows him a different side of who he is."

"Jung says we have a thousand selves...."

"More."

\* \* \*

Harry would sit down, say, "tell me a joke," and I'd say, for example, "I was having dinner with my father when I made a Freudian slip. I meant to say, *Please pass the mashed potatoes.* Instead I said, *You motherfucker, you ruined my whole life.*"

Harry would laugh, loud enough that Freud would have been pleased. Freud says the kinds of jokes we laugh at expose our repressed wishes and longings.

"Did your father ruin your whole life?" I asked.

"No, I think it was war."

"This word, I've never heard at Emporio Rulli."

"Should I tell you a story?"

"I don't know."

"I'm out on this hill in the dark with a bunch of soldiers. My buddy and I are trying to locate a target, where the shooting is coming from. He can see it and he points into the blackness, but I see nothing. He lines up his rifle, puts his cheek against mine, and tells me he's going to shift his head a little to the left and I should look. He moves his head, just a little, to the left, and at that exact moment … comes the bullet … that kills him…."

Harry looked into my devastated eyes. "It was stunning, Jewel, so quick, no suffering."

\* \* \*

I didn't want to go out on September twelfth. The day after 9/11, like everyone else, I was in shock. I went to the café because it was my habit. How else were we to behave, now that Americans were revealed as vulnerable, not invincible but targets, in the sightlines of a many-tentacled beast?

Harry was reading the *New York Times* at an outside table. I was stopped still on the sidewalk by the stacked photos of before-and-after skylines, showing where other large buildings surrounding the World Trade Centers had also collapsed, a striking record of the scope of the change. Harry was sitting with a very tall blonde wearing a red shawl and white turtleneck, lots of bracelets, a silver cross necklace. Her eyes were that clear, clairvoyant blue of the pure-at-heart. Of course they were talking about terrorism. She was supplying platitudes while Harry was knocking holes in her willingness to be comforted by notions such as spirit that cannot be broken, or government able to step up and represent our best interests, that the best in human nature was bound to prevail, especially in the face of surprise attacks from invisible evil.

Harry proposed (quoting Nietzsche, maybe) that total destruction might be necessary before good could re-emerge. Elsa disagreed, arguing that the world's goodness remained intact.

"Yes, but it will have to strike back, commit murder, and that goes against the nature of goodness."

I brought over my cappuccino, sat with them, and listened. Others came, drank coffee, contributed to the dialog, went on their way; we remained. Finally, Harry introduced me to Elsa, noting that we both had written books about the death of a child. Mine an infant with extreme brain damage, hers a two-year-old with cancer. Our stories entered the café on the same day war was declared. A young woman wearing skinny white jeans and high-heeled sandals, newly arrived, sat next to Harry unspeaking while Elsa and I went blow by blow with our experiences: diagnosis, responses, treatment, the law, the challenge of making ethical decisions in the face of such enemies.

She had killed her daughter with "a morphine bullet."

I had gradually withdrawn mine from artificial feeding, "starved her to death."

We had justifiable reasons.

*We were both merciful.*

*We were both murderers.*

We had waged war, learned the enormity of

what we were fighting, taken action. Our goal was peace, via death, in our arms, at home.

Harry said this conversation was depressing, while his young mistress quietly pondered whether such a thing could ever happen to her.

In the face of the next war Elsa and I were veterans, calm, knew what to do.

Resist *and* surrender.

Be still *and* keep moving.

Love everything enduring *and* impermanent: music, talk, the beasts, the café, life.

\* \* \*

Next time I saw him, Harry wanted to lend me a memoir he thought I should read and invited me to follow him home. He located the book then showed me around, downstairs to his grand piano. I was wearing my yoga sweats, mandala tee shirt, spa sandals; he had on tennis shorts and sneakers. He seated himself at the piano and played. I studied the book cover, his hands as they stroked the keys, and the strong muscles of his legs as he pumped the foot pedals. Music filled the sunny morning air and there was no evidence of beasts. They were either in lockdown, vanquished, or we had learned to live in peace with their presence among us.

## Raven

*You might say the streets flow sweetly
through the night.*
~ Xavier Villaurutia, *Nostalgia for Death*

David, Richie, and Raven were all together
in San Miguel de Allende because Raven lived
here now, and Raven was dying. I met David
and Richie one night at Tio Lucas bar midway
through their visit. Next day Raven drove past
the three of us out walking in town and asked
them later, *who's the babe?* It'd been years since
Lee called me *Babe,* and I liked it. We had one
week. This created a glow around us, intensity
to our time together that was a miniature, more
frivolous mirror of Raven's urgency. At the same
time, we felt no hurry; the days were long.

I came here on my winter break from teaching
and had created a schedule for myself because
routines helped me feel more stable alone. The
first few days I kept busy writing on my hotel
balcony but the unfamiliar freedom of being away
left me wandering streets or sitting in restaurants

at odd times of day. I was learning new rhythms, the pace of the place: write early, Bellas Artes for cappuccino around 10, walk, visit the *jardin* around noon, Posada de las Monjas for *siesta:* nap, read, write, meet hotel neighbors, until at least past 7. Then slowly the nighttime streets of the cobblestone town came to life. Everyone gathered at the *jardin,* walking through or sitting on benches to watch the people go by. Teenagers and twenty-somethings were here to study Spanish, art, or Mexican culture. Worldly, retired Americans and Canadians came to escape winter or empty love lives, stretch dollars, or possibly, become someone else once more. In their midst: me at midlife, *newlyunwed,* traveling alone, for one week.

The night I met David and Richie I had been to a poetry reading (per schedule), was invited to join the poets for dinner but couldn't handle the "group dynamics" and slipped away to Tio Lucas. I sat at David and Richie's table in the bar where they were waiting to be called for dinner but they didn't notice me. They were here for Raven and each other, plus (I later learned) they had wives at home and were practicing, after a number of lost marriages and relationships, being faithful men.

They paused from talking and found me there, "trying not to eavesdrop."

"You grew up in New Jersey?"

"You're Jews from New York? My ex is a Jew from Long Island!"

"You dance salsa? Let's go dancing."

We all had been at the same Ravi Shankar/ George Harrison concert at Madison Square Garden in the '70s! It was like we'd known each other for years! I didn't know which one to like more! Then their table was called and they politely went off to eat. Then Richie returned to invite me to join them, and so I did.

We discussed the menu, jazz, San Miguel, Raven, their wives, my ex, the midlife crisis.

One said it's real; the other, not.

David called it, "Road not taken."

Richie said, "Insatiable desire."

I offered, "Paradise lost?"

David said, "Jung's shadow."

I told the story of Ricardo, the married

Mexican Texan I'd met at my hotel two nights before. "He's 40 years old with a toddler and a pregnant wife and comes knocking on the door to my room at midnight, begging: *abre la puerta.* Good thing, *no* is the same word in English and Spanish."

After *ceviche,* more *margaritas, arroz con pollo, carne y verduras, huitlacochtle* (tasty black fungus mushrooms), and one shared *helado* dessert we agreed to meet in the morning, for cappuccino at Bellas Artes at 10.

The whole next day we walked the cobblestones, up and down the steep hills and stairs, studying views, a museum, *tiendas,* eating, drinking, talking. We kept meeting every day, falling in love with the place and each other.

\* \* \*

On the fifth day Richie had to take Raven to the hospital and David and I sat out the afternoon and twilight on my hotel rooftop, chatting, sipping *damiana,* and smoking, close to an increasingly starlit sky, listening to music all over town, church bells, dogs barking, dialogs on streets below, hotel guests coming and going.

Inside, we talked on opposite twin beds until three in the morning.

The air was charged after all the days and hours of languorous, revealing, verbal intercourse. Tonight we had covered (among other things) erotic poetry, the clitoris, his first fumbling experience with a college girlfriend, how it "didn't work" and he went to the library to "study up" and they took their time and talked themselves through it until they were mutually satisfied.

"I now consider myself a pretty good lover," he admitted, and described his wife's body to me. "She's not the type of woman I usually go for. They'd be more like you."

I contained my longing, as he debated his "moral dilemma."

With no more talking he moved us into a standing-up, very tentative hug-then-kiss where our bodies sensed each other, what it would be like, and our lips reached and searched and also held back before he pulled away then I said, "I'll step back and make it easy for you to leave, how's that?"

I took the step. And he left.

I went to bed with our desire: desire alone, pleasing, mutual, alive.

\* \* \*

On my last afternoon in town I finally met Raven. The four of us sat at an outdoor table at the edge of the *jardin* and watched the people pass.

Richie said, "Ever heard the saying, *man with many hats?*" and pointed to a young Mexican selling straw hats, stacked on top of his head, reaching all the way to the sky. A marionette clown wheeled by on his little bicycle, mariachi music drifted around a corner, bells clanged forth from the *parroquia* tower, sun rays penetrated wispy clouds like spread fingers from divine hands.

Throat cancer made Raven's voice quiet, head bowed into his neck as if surgery had reduced the distance or his ability to stretch up. David, Richie, and I ordered beer; Raven couldn't join in because he had to consume everything through a tube. But he begged to taste and did so with a spoon then dribbled and reached for a napkin to wipe his mouth. When he spoke he was the local, and we leaned toward him to hear him better, the knowledgeable one with much to say, even as his body was slowly, as he spoke, deserting him.

"Enjoy this," he was saying.

The old, hideous, guitar man strolled by our table and handed us a card with song titles: *Cielito Lindo, La Bamba, Guantanamera,* etcetera.

I handed the card to Raven: "You choose."

But he couldn't focus on the hand-printed words. All during our time together I watched him struggle to remain in the world with us, as he contemplated leaving it, still in his body, coughing, dribbling, uncomfortable in his posture. He knew he was dying, while David, Richie, and I fancied ourselves in the middle of life, and savored the scene, the sun, beer, good company, blissful in our bodies' passions, hungers, and thirsts.

So we were able to pay attention to the ugly old troubadour as he sang through his stained, crumbling teeth:

> *que bonito el cielo*
> *que bonita la luz*
> *que bonito es el amor*
> *~ in memory of Raven*

## Love Is Blind in One Eye

I gazed through the window of Piazza
d'Angelo at the standing-room-only crowd of
beautiful people, then with trepidation boldly
entered the bar and inserted myself in their
midst: Mill Valley affluent, fit, knew their wines,
especially the California varietals. The chatter
level was high and I tried to grasp the train of
conversation so I could leap on. A lot of it was
stocks. And tennis, renovations, best golf resorts
on Maui, favorite Club Med spots. I was there
fresh from a Book Passage reading on a Thursday
at 8, too wired to go home and be alone. A soccer
game played on three TVs behind the bar then
the day's news about sinkholes on the Richmond
Bridge (over which I commuted), and the ongoing
quest to capture Osama bin Laden, dead or alive.

The man standing to my right had a gorgeous
profile. I liked the way he wore his collared
shirts one over the other. He looked solid and
comfortable, with the *Chronicle* folded and
tucked under his arm. He ordered *pinot grigio,*
that exotic name.

He asked what brought me here.

"To be around people," I told him.

"Plenty of people here."

"Don't they have families?"

"Maybe not."

"Don't you?"

"Not exactly."

"You have a family!"

"I live with my son and daughter."

"Not their mother?"

"We're in the middle of a war." (For a second I thought he was referring to Bin Laden, whose bearded face had appeared in multiple on the bar TVs.)

"I know what you mean."

"It's a nightmare."

And so we commenced to tell war stories in the middle of the happy, crowded scene.

A seat opened up at the bar, I sat down, and the warrior moved closer. This side of his face appeared newly wrinkled, maybe in the last year or so. The eye I could see was green. His outer collar was turned up over his freckled neck; dark chest hairs curled through the unbuttoned opening of his denim shirt; the sleeve of the dark wool overshirt brushed my shoulder.

His wife wanted everything he had: house, car, children.

"She's jobless."

He believed she was suicidal.

He wanted to do the right thing.

But maintain his right to his share.

"All the money came from me: my inheritance bought the first house, my investments paid it off, I have worked my butt off, I love my kids and I want to be their father."

"I'm sure she wants that, too."

"No. She wants me to pay for everything and be invisible."

"That doesn't sound fair."

"I've been paying lawyers for three years."

This was actually the first time he had "stepped out at night like this," too defeated by the process to imagine he could have any kind of life apart from supporting children, his wife's insanity, and attorneys. He's been living in studio apartments but finally just put everything into this new house.

"Where?"

"Here."

"So, you're doing all right."

"We're working with a mediator now. I'm a little more hopeful."

He couldn't even face me, he was so mired in his situation, and then suddenly politeness compelled him to ask me about myself.

"Name's Art, by the way. You are?"

"Jewel."

"Pretty. So what's your story?"

"We're done with paperwork, no assets to fight over."

"Kids?"

"One dead, one living, best kid ever."

Compared to Art, my split with Lee was downright amicable. He dropped off and picked up Dale when he said he would, deposited a tiny sum each month into our old joint account for child support (thank you), was holding his job, not threatening me with anything. I only suffered from the withdrawal of his love. And even that, I was getting used to; it wasn't like a knife anymore, more like a spoon, my body yielding to it like ice cream left standing on the counter.

\* \* \*

More wine and in between new and old stories in the middle of all the noise, Art started describing an old family photograph that showed his childhood family still intact: his mother, father, and their two children. Their summer cabin was visible in the background. The family posed on the dock on the shore of the lake. The afternoon was sunny. Everyone was smiling, healthy, young, their futures ahead.

Art and his big brother Steve were four and five, their parents in their late twenties. That night at dinner the big brother got mad at the little brother, as he often did, and with no more intent to do permanent damage than ever before, Steve aimed, then threw his fork as hard as he could across the table. Everyone watched in slow motion as the object hurtled through the short distance and the sharp tines caught the little brother in the right eye. It was fast, even in slow motion, and the impulsive action inflicted damage that would never go away. The boy was blind in one eye for the rest of his life.

"Not long after that day my mother was diagnosed with polio and got increasingly disabled until she died when I was twelve. My father was devastated, and had to let the cabin go, which had been in my mother's family for generations. My brother was eternally guilty and became self-destructive in all the usual ways: drinking, smoking, and driving too fast, and was killed in a car accident at age nineteen."

Of them all, the blind boy fared best. Found music. Married, had a family. Did well financially. Learned to adjust his profile so his best side was seen.

Art turned to face me then and I could see his white, blind eye.

\* \* \*

A week later we met for coffee, his son skateboarded around the Mill Valley plaza where we talked, the morning passed, and I fell in love with them both. We sat talking for hours while the boy came and went around us. Art wanted to hear about me, my turn to tell stories, he said, and he listened more attentively than most men, as if to compensate for the eye that couldn't see. I told him I'd published a book, a memoir about my baby who died, called *Silvie's Life*.

"I'd like to read it," Art said.

*With one eye?* I thought, laughing, looking forward to a relationship unfolding, where we would tell each other all our stories, set ourselves free, make peace with the past. Bombs were falling all over the world, our enemies were invisible, among us; maybe there was no peace to be had. But they say love is blind: it can overlook the devastated past, crawl through half-seeing darkness, dare to peer into a hopeful future.

I never saw him again.

His good eye liked me but his blind eye couldn't see beyond his wars.

## Alive in Lisbon

*The lights have come on, the night is falling,*
*life changes its face.*
*One way or another I have to keep on living.*
*My soul burns like a hand, physically.*
*I'm on the road of all men and they bump*
*against me.*
~ Fernando Pessoa

My hotel is as I pictured it, simple with all the comforts: nice bed, private bath (with bidet and tub), phone, desk, and best: terrace and wide-angle view of the red-tiled roofs of the vast city of Lisbon. The light of late afternoon is soft-focus and otherworldly. At night circus/calliope rhythms reach my windows from a courtyard below, where a large group of teenagers practice a line dance: march, grapevine, side-step, swing your partner, singing along in Portuguese.

Leaving in the morning on foot from the inn's hilltop perch near Miradouro do Monte means following a winding path downhill through Graça and Alfama's narrow neighborhood streets.

Looking into doorways, walking the cobbled alleys, I lose track of how to retrace my steps, and can only go forward, on a self-paced stroll with no destination. Glimpses of Tagus River provide orientation and I head toward the water to gain my bearings. My new beaded sandals work well on the stones: stable ground. Knee-length skirt a comfort, glad to have sweater on turns into sudden gusts. I walk along the wide riverfront boulevard toward Municipal Plaza, and now I appreciate the comfort of being where tourists are expected. The pedestrian shopping street, Rua Agosto, leads to Rossio Plaza and a stop for *cafe con natas* at a sidewalk cafe for people watching.

I sit among street musicians, beggars, tourists, and artists. Here I am, author of *Silvie's Life,* story of the life and death of my baby girl, now a book adopted for courses on end-of-life ethics and the right to die, translated into Portuguese. My publisher has invited me to speak at four venues in Portugal, and agreed to pay my flight and three nights hotel but I have no cheque in hand yet, and so I worry a little about everything.

I observe the Human Statue at work nearby

his collection jar, standing on a high box, white garb draped at length so he appears extra tall, in white face, white hands, cloth wrapped like gauze, facial expression of a sad clown. A crowd gathers, awaiting his act. But the act is simply this: to stand perfectly still, be like Pessoa, no one, empty, a blank canvas on whom the observer can toss a personality, empty so perhaps a soul can appear.

At the corner: a mysterious figure seated on a doorstep: Is he wearing a mask? What does it signify? What does he mean for us to make of it, to think?

A closer look reveals that it is the man's face, his actual face! Visible purple and red tumors, bursting vessels twice as big as his face, grow there, obscuring his humanity. Attempting to understand what I'm seeing, I catch his eye, barely detectible amidst the raw, red clay of his face.

*He has eyes! He's human!*

Not soulless like the white-draped statue, but fully present, and stricken by this disease, his fate, which renders him a beggar. Who could love such a being? I do, I love him; the eye connects his humanity to mine. I drop all my coins and bills in his upturned palm then join a stream of others passing by him without stopping.

Later, I describe him to my doctor hosts and learn it's true, there's nothing medicine can do for his particular affliction. The society of neonatologists wants to know why this is so: why do some newborns arrive with *anomalias* – defects, predispositions, imbalances – that will render their lives miserable or short, or both?

Death is everyone's fate, but the whims and will of expected natural order include this percentage of chaos and extremes at the edges of commonness.

Doctors do not respond with the "why" of philosophy, literature, or religion; they face off anomalies with science, analyze statistics for where and why there arise clusters of experience, use microscopes to examine close-up the details of the misshaped kidney, trace back in sonograms to which prenatal period initiates the "wrong turn," present findings in PowerPoint in darkened hotel conference rooms (as outside the sun blazes, wind pushes air, waves pound the rocky Viana do Castelo coast). The audience takes notes. Where can the doctor intervene to prevent this, or if not, to treat it, to right the wrong? Research is assessed, conclusions offered: these are the possibilities; this is what we might be able to control. The rest – what is out of control – is not the subject of these meetings.

I'm introduced into the conversation to tell my story. The title of my memoir has been translated as *Estar Grávida É Estar de Esperanças:* "Being pregnant is called expecting," the first sentence of *Silvie's Life*. I read from a chapter set in the Neonatal Intensive Care Unit (NICU), a place I call "God out of control," and my book says, "This is not supposed to happen."

My daughter's case was extreme. After ten days of tests, trauma, and assessment, her doctors concluded she had suffered severe brain damage and that death was "her best hope." Our task as parents became how to allow for this within the boundaries of law, morality, our deep love for her, and our pointless wish for her to come to life and thrive.

"We needed an explanation. No one could explain it," I read.

Does the distinguished lady doctor wearing the cross necklace cringe when I call God out of control? *Silvie's Life* wonders what kind of faith can allow for belief in a God who designs *anomalias,* or, if not designs them, permits them to exist?

Belief that suggests this is part of our lesson here?

Imperfection.

Only God is perfect? – and maybe even God is still learning.

\* \* \*

The churches of Portugal are fortresses, walls three feet thick, interiors a kind of hubris, prideful reaching toward some perceived, conferred power – priests' throne-like seats, bishops' tombs, velvet robes, worship-me rituals. I feel both awe and cynicism inside these monuments to power.

The University of Coimbra's grand plaza overlooks the city and river, and to step inside the ancient library requires an appointment. My group enters the temperature-controlled, sacred space with its ladders to high shelves, books in cages, grand conformity of spines and colors, grand depository of knowledge on medicine, law, physics, mathematics, the arts. Climbing through the buildings, the steps are unevenly sunken and slippery from thousands of footprints, weight of centuries; I can feel my fleeting presence and my permanent mark as well.

\* \* \*

At Cafe Brasileira in Lisbon, Portugal's most famous poet, Fernando Pessoa, is honored in the form of a bronze statue of a man in a hat and suit seated at a bronze outdoor café table, with an empty seat beside him where everyone who passes feels compelled to sit and pose for photos. I regard this parade: the traveler observes, the writer records these observations, the ordinary person wants her picture taken with Pessoa, and I hand my camera to a café neighbor, gesturing the shutter click as we don't speak the same language.

Then I enter the café and head toward the back to watch all the comings and goings. All is chatter, animated, relaxed, nothing going on that doesn't happen here on any given afternoon, when I see four men enter through the front doorway; one pushes the other, who returns a punch to the shoulder, which causes the first one to stumble then retaliate. Portuguese is tossed in the air, some insult or threat, then the four go at it, a regular *brouhaha,* and the patrons shout, stand up from their seats (myself among them), as the tinkle of breaking glass is heard – the mirror at the entrance? glass in the doors? port glasses at tables? A roar goes up, the waiters shout, one hurls a bottle at them, the bartender is on the phone to *Policia* as is the fat lady on her cell.

Outside, there's a row of sidewalk cafés full of people who leap up shouting as the men "take it outside," and proceed with the fight down the block.

Inside, the café settles into an excited bustle – Ah, how the energy of the afternoon can change, the moment of danger reinvigorates the ordinary; emotional tenor shifts.

We've just dodged "what could have happened" (one pulls a gun, or the tumble falls in my direction; I am, after all, trapped in the back of the café, the fight at its entrance; we were all forced to witness and wait to see where danger might strike, be prepared to defend our space and lives). Everyone is shaking their heads, reliving excitement, speculating, dismissing the men as ruffians, laughing about it now; fear gone and replaced with some new elation that coffee and wine can't offer. Only the adrenalin of fear gives this spark.

\* \* \*

At my hotel I overhear the clerk, Jose Manuel, describing his "problem child." Later, we talk to each other and I show him my book: "This is why I'm here." (He speaks some English; I employ my little Portuguese.) Soon, he is pulling pictures from his wallet, one of his son now at age five, and the dreaded NICU shot with the newborn attached to all the tubes and wearing the too-familiar cap and blanket with the same pink and turquoise stripes used in the States.

I gulp. "Yes, my baby looked like this. But listen, her situation was extreme. She didn't live."

His baby, his boy, lives, and his challenges will be ongoing (I don't diagnose but it sounds like autism, or obsessive-compulsive disorder; Jose Manuel says *hyperactive)*. He and his wife disagree about how to respond, and I worry for their marriage; I've been through all this, death and divorce, and feel like I'm on the other side. I have Dale, my strapping lad, and many blessings: good work, great health, many communities.

I point to Teresa Botelho's name in the preface to *Estar Grávida É Estar de Esperanças,* "Maybe she can help you; she works with these children and families."

Jose Manuel has no faith in psychologists, he says, he doesn't read books, but accepts my gift of the book, maybe for his wife.

\* \* \*

On Monday morning I'm scheduled to tour the public hospital with Teresa Botelho, Maria do Ceu Machado, who wrote the other preface, and Alexandra Dias, my translator. Dr. Machado heads the Department of Pediatrics and Neonatology; Dr. Botelho leads the psychology team; Dr. Dias is a respected pediatrician.

Two young psychologists-in-training accompany us as we visit the children's library and play room, staff offices, wards, and intensive care. We pass through waiting rooms for day service appointments, noisy with hordes of the needy, all races.

It is a squelching hot day and the hospital is not an air-conditioned place; the air is stifling with the smell of bodies, illness, and fear. On the wards, there is the smell of bleach and disinfectants; in the cafeteria, hospital food. My hosts, used to the smells, the air, the sight of the needy hordes, walk past as if guiding me through a cathedral or museum, casually (kindly, respectfully) pointing out children with pneumonia, those with long-term care needs, one with possible lymphoma or is it edema that will respond to medication given one more day?

All is well, *tudo bem,* I'm in stride, okay, until I'm invited in, inside, in closer, to see the newborns in their cubicles. Alone in a blanketed cubby, there's Matilda, teeny, bruised, connected by wires, holding on by a thread, alive. Breathing!

I bend close to peer inside, a spectator, and feel ashamed for looking, for being on tour.

Gulps of emotion are swallowed then rise like air as I cross the room to meet the young Portuguese mother hovering lovingly over her perfectly beautiful baby boy. He is so so small, desperately yet calmly attempting to live with his intricate hands and complex brain waves, internal organs striving to do their work of coming into life and sustaining life before he is fully formed and ready. He's been here three months so far. This mother has been here, too, in this darkened room with the busy nurses, doctors, and monitors, in love with this new being, faithfully conjuring hopeful thoughts.

This is when I start to cry, seeing that young mother. Looking into the more dire condition of the fist-sized African preemie, grasping a hand in camaraderie with the stoic, broad mother, I mumble, *"Compreendo,* I understand." I want to offer hopeful prayers, can only extend my empathy.

As we exit, a deep well of old feelings engulfs me as I fall, weeping, down the well.

My guides seem surprised and I am, too.

"It's been 18 years, I didn't expect to feel this

way, I'm sorry."

"You haven't been in a NICU since?"

"No."

*Why would I?*

I ran as far from the place as I could get, avoided all thoughts of this becoming my life's work. Yet I wrote *Silvie's Life,* and attention was being paid to her story, again, after all these years, and it is my work here now.

One neonatologist down the hall realizes it's me, the famous author, here in their midst, and hurries over, drops everything to catch up with me, to tell me, *this is an important book* – she read it last week on a plane, because she heard I would be here – how meaningful it is for doctors to hear the whole story from the patient's side of the bed.

Someone has brought me tissues and I stand in the hallway dabbing at eye makeup, as I try to absorb this praise. Aware I could sob all day, bottomless buckets even after all this time, I recuperate enough to move through the cafeteria line with these fine people, swallow a few mouthfuls of bad food, attempt to keep track of conversation about the newest baby in crisis.

* * *

My other appointment on my last day in Lisbon is at the offices of Gradiva Publishers with the formal Sr. Begonha, who has most efficiently arranged for my cheque. Generous Sr. Begonha inquires how I'll spend the rest of the day.

"Wander your neighborhood, drink coffee; try to process everything that's happened."

Sr. Begonha locates a city map and highlights his recommended path to tranquility, then walks me to the corner and his favorite café, points downhill to *Jardin do Estrela* (with its beautiful, shaded benches to rest on, gazebo, and wide walking paths), and beyond to his secret garden – *Jardin Botanica,* an oasis of palm trees, labyrinth hedges, and giant-root, ancient *arbols*. There, in the silence at the center of Lisbon city, I will find a shaded bench and release all my tears, shed mascara, snot, and façades of composure.

I will cry for many reasons, not least my shock that my deceased baby girl herself has led me here, to this dark green garden. *Silvie,* her fictional name, connects to the word *sylvan,* meaning, green dark forest. *Aha.* Her mother will smile at the image of herself weeping wetly in the garden in the city of Lisbon, so far away from home; she'll blow her nose, wipe sweat, persist in walking through the heat onward toward the rest of her life.

\* \* \*

Back at the hotel I pay my bill with the Gradiva cheque, shy around José Manuel. Business settled, he says, "I read your book today."

"The whole book?"

"Yes. In three sessions. I had to stop when guests arrived, of course, and when I cried."

His experience was exactly the same in the beginning, he tells me; it brought all the memories back. "But of course my son is alive, and for that I can be grateful."

Guests come in and need his attention. Jose Manuel nods to me, embraces my hand, and I bow good night. *Boa noite.*

I ride the elevator to the rooftop bar and buy two bottles of water to drink in my room while I ponder the nighttime view. Outside, the calliope dance loudly proceeds.

# 12 Hours in Barcelona

The flight from Palma, Mallorca, Spain, to San Francisco, California, included a long layover in Barcelona. I landed in the city of Gaudi at 6pm and would be on another plane from the same airport at dawn. I could easily have "killed time" at the huge airport: shopped, ate, read, slept in uncomfortable chairs. I considered dropping some Euros on a hotel in town. But why kill time, when time is all I have?

I place my luggage in a large airport locker and get on a bus to the center of the city. No plan, except to see where in the world I am tonight.

I've been to big cities: New York, LA, London, Lisbon, Paris, Mexico DF. Barcelona, too, is huge, a sprawl, with miles of concrete and uncountable numbers of people. Twelve hours had seemed like a really long time and now I see it is a single half-moon on the face of the ever-cycling clock of eternity. No amount of time could be enough to absorb what is here: true of any lifetime, in any place: never enough time.

But I try.

I see right away that I will not be able to cover much ground on foot. The blocks are long, the buildings loom, imposing shadows and blocking views. The double-decker red city tour bus pulls into line at the downtown square and I become exactly what I am: a tourist here.

I step up with the others and pay the price for a guided drive through the city on the open-air upper level of the bus. Three beautiful young British men help me with the headphones and point out where we are on the map: a dot inside interlocking circles. They have tour-bus passes that allow them to step on and off buses for three full days: stay, linger, view, walk, hop back on elsewhere, return each day for more. I will not be here long enough to make full use of my one-day pass, just long enough to take full advantage during this fortuitous, out-of-time interlude in Spain.

Dusk in Barcelona. September. The air is perfect. I am dressed just right with a light sweater. And I am alone in the world.

\* \* \*

Mallorca, too, was an interlude. Yachting

around the island, six of us, three couples. I was part of that, coupled for the week. I made the captain happy, I smiled, was pretty; we bantered, got drunk, took off our clothes, made love in the V berth. Separate people, back home he and I had been dating maybe a year, broke up, got back in touch, got together a few times a week now, otherwise on our own. A loose arrangement, desirable for those who've been burned by love, still paying for the last arrangement, smarting, on guard; meeting new mates, we proceed without commitments, with caution, so the heart won't break again if this, too, should end. Must all love end? All lives end. We pass through, touch down, connect for a moment, move on, leave so much behind. And it matters so little, our cracked little hearts, in the grand scope of things? Big Barcelona makes that obvious. I pass hundreds of couples out on the town, fighting and kissing.

The coupling was good but I had to get back to California, to teaching. I'd already played enough hooky at the start of the new school year. My guy was staying on, renting a Ducati and motorcycling through the Pyrenees for another week. I was invited to join him for that as well. But there was school. And I also knew he'd be happier alone on his bike in the landscape. He is happiest alone. I understood that; it was not something about him that could be changed. We had our week, glorious, then we kissed goodbye at the yacht harbor and I tried to leave any feelings of wanting more from him there.

*Is this true of myself as well? Am I happiest alone?*

\* \* \*

The dusky light gives way to streetlights on the gaudy Gaudi structures erected incomprehensibly in the middle of, next to, juxtaposed with, the surrounding architecture that looks nothing alike. Where were the city planners when this city was built? Barcelona is a wild conglomeration of architectural styles, shapes, heights, and colors. I breathe it in, adjust my eyes to the shifting twilight, move the tiny headphone buds deeper into my ears to learn the history, where to focus my eyes and thoughts, as we pass through this chaos of sights-to-see.

I hear bits and pieces:

*The Olympics were here in _____.*
*There is the Jewish Hill....*
*The     _____     Museum,     _____     Library,*
*_____ Theatre.*

In the giant downtown gazebo, are those Russian ballerinas pirouetting?

A series of fountains spew color-lit water bursts in sequence to a Bartók symphony!

Now, fireworks explode into skies between buildings.

Hundreds, no *thousands,* of people are out walking the streets.

Wow, Barcelona! It is ALIVE! Is every night like this?

No, of course not. I happen to have a 12-hour layover in Barcelona on a festival occasion, a night when free ballets and symphonies and theatrical performances are taking place all over town, lending a glow, heightening our pleasure, focusing the eye out of the chaos of so-much-to-see into the framework of the arts: dance, music, language. Over there, young spoken-word poets are rapping hip-hop beats; here, it's Shakespeare in Spanish; now, a celebratory speech; in my ear, the stories of Barcelona's past and future. I see it all from my perch on top of this slow-moving red bus.

* * *

Having circled one loop of city highlights, I step off the bus and enter the strolling crowd of pedestrians on La Rambla. On any night of the year, I had heard, what you do most especially in Barcelona is walk La Rambla with its outdoor cafés, restaurants, shops, and galleries. It is nighttime now and I am on my own in the teeming city, fearless.

*I have walked on fire.*

The worst things I could have imagined when I was a naïve and arrogant young woman all have happened: robberies, rape, death of my baby girl, death of my marriage, death of myths of how life is supposed to be. There's no such thing as supposed-to-be! I know this now. There is only HOW IT IS and (like Barcelona) life is like this: chaotic, unpredictable, dynamic. And, it is also orderly (like symphonies and ballets), predictable (there will always be hundreds of pedestrians walking La Rambla), and energized (life is forceful, changeable).

I've changed. I never thought I'd feel this kind of free joy again, this loose/liberated ability to couple and part, this independent willingness to enter the stream of strangers, strong, happy, one of them.

&ast; &ast; &ast;

Near midnight I find a pleasing restaurant – a clean, well-lighted place – with more people than you'd think would be out dining at midnight (unlike at home, where everyone is ready for bed by 8pm, my bedroom community of early commuters and high achievers).

I order red wine and a bowl of soup. The bread arrives with the wine and I serve myself my own holy communion. I chat with a Dutch man dining alone at the next table. He's living here for a month, studying art and Spanish.

"How long are you here for?" he asks.

"Twelve hours. And it's half-over."

We smile and talk across the space between us as we eat, then I head back out into the streets and join the crowd.

Half over, like life? Not over yet.

## Acknowledgments

*The author wishes to thank the editors who*
*previously published these stories:*

Firewalking: *Sideshow* (1997)
Someplace Else: *Sideshow* (1992)
Emporio Rulli: *RedbridgeReview.co.uk*
(Summer 2006)
Raven: *The Best Travel Writing 2006*
(Travelers Tales)
Love Is Blind in One Eye: *ChickLitReview.org*
(January 2007)
Alive in Lisbon: *The Best Women's Travel*
*Writing 2008* (Travelers Tales)
12 Hours in Barcelona: *The Best Travel Writing*
*2010* (Travelers Tales)

*This is a collection of short fiction, except for*
*Travelers Tales stories, which are nonfiction.*

## About the Author

Marianne Rogoff is the author of the memoir *Silvie's Life* (Zenobia Press, Berkeley, 1995; Gradiva, Lisbon, 2006), which has been adopted for courses in medical ethics and optioned for film. Travelers Tales has published her stories in *The Best Women's Travel Writing* (2011, 2010, 2008) and *The Best Travel Writing* (2006). Her feature essays and book reviews have appeared in *The Rumpus, San Francisco Chronicle,* and *Bloomsbury Review,* among others. She teaches Writing & Literature at California College of the Arts and Big History at Dominican University, and leads annual weeklong trips for writers to Mexico, Spain, and elsewhere. Read more at **mariannerogoff.com**

## shebooks
www.Shebooks.net